MY NAME IS *Kim*

SANDRA FAIR

Published by Silversmith Press–Houston, Texas
www.silversmithpress.com

978-1-967386-51-2 Softcover
978-1-967386-69-7 Hardcover
978-1-967386-67-3 Ebook

To those finding the

courage to begin—including myself.

For my family,

who taught me it's okay to start again from anywhere.

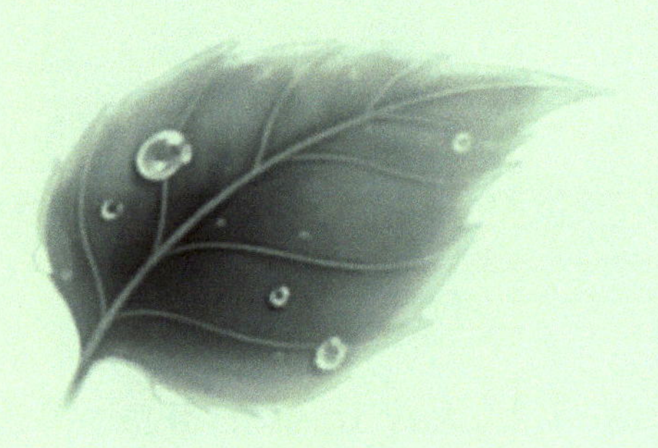

In the corner of the old university lot stood a lonesome tree by itself. It looked like a portrait that had withstood the test of time—tall and majestic against the sky. Its leaves fell like long strands of hair over muscled branches and weathered bark.

Its roots crawled outward like ancient fingers, deeply embedded in the earth, surrounded by a quiet garden of flowers—as if paying homage to a great king that once ruled the world.

And yet the tree remained, perfectly in tune with its surroundings, so seamlessly woven into the landscape that most no longer noticed it at all.

Time had not broken it.

Time had simply muted it.

But the tree remembered.

Beneath its stillness, beneath rings carved by decades of sun and storm, old memories stirred.

Once, wishes had risen through its branches like sparks.

Desperate ones. Hopeful ones. Innocent ones.

Lately, they come differently.

They were light, barely touching the air before dissolving.

They asked for more without knowing why.

For things that glittered briefly and faded just as fast.

The tree felt no weight in them.

No roots.

No life.

Words were spoken, but hearts remained guarded.

And so, the wishes fell away—unfinished, unanswered, forgotten almost as soon as they were made.

The tree did not deny them.

It simply could not awaken for what carried no truth.

My name is Kim.

I chose that name because I like it. I was once like you, living each day like there's no tomorrow. Back then, you always came seeking my company.

Children once dared each other to swing from my lower limbs. Lovers claimed my shade in the late afternoons, whispering sweet nothings that felt larger than the world.

Some days, someone would lie against my trunk and take a nap, cap over their face, and rest from the worries of the world.

In spring, birds would nest deep within my branches, their songs weaving through chatter from afar. In summer, cicadas hummed until the air felt thick with sound. After rain, frogs gathered near my roots, hidden but alive, their small movements stirring the damp earth.

I held them all.

I was never empty.

I am simply a part of things, constantly there, so few of you would think to look twice.

The best part of it all is having a good night's sleep to end yesterday's sorrow and waking up each day, fresh and ready for a brand-new day."

I do not know if you remember me.

It has been a long time since I felt the warmth of the sun or heard laughter that stayed.

I have always been here—through rain and drought,

Through wind that bent everything but me.

Lightning and thunder have no power over me.

Floodwaters have served as my great bounty, leaving me luscious and greener than ever.

Once, you came to me freely.

You rested in my shade.

You carved out promises into my bark.

You whispered wishes beneath blue skies while my leaves fluttered in anticipation.

You only have to ask, and it shall be yours.

I answered what was true.

Wishes that came from the heart, I have no right to turn them away.

You were there, when the sky was blue, and all my friends celebrated with you.

In those days, I felt vast. I felt invincible.

The world has grown louder since then.

Buildings rise where forests once stood.

Eyes lower toward glowing screens instead of looking at the sky.

Now, with all that is left,

You don't look at me anymore.

I feel ridiculously invisible in this new world.

I simply remain.

Waiting.

For a wish that carries weight again.

My name is Kim.

I once believed you would return.

Many of you left in search of something brighter,

Something louder—something promised beyond the horizon.

I cannot follow you where you go.

I offer shade to the weary.

Silence to the overwhelmed.

A place where breath can slow and settle.

I have always been here.

The modern world dazzles you now.

It moves quickly.

It fills your hands and your hours.

I do not compete with it.

But I feel the distance.

My branches still stretch wide.

My leaves still listen.

My roots still wait for what carries weight.

I still feel your heart.

I am powerful in one way,

I answer what's true in your heart.

And truth cannot be forced.

Yet I stand.

I remember when I was not alone.

There were others once—trees whose branches touched mine in the wind.

We marked the seasons together. We listened to the same sky.

I do not know when they disappeared. It happened slowly.

And slowly, the world changed.

Where green once gathered, gray now stands.

Where roots once intertwined, roads were paved.

Yet I remain.

The world moves differently now.

It moves with certainty that I do not share.

I am old in a way that does not easily fit here.

There was a time when wishes were made with faith unguarded.

When the heart spoke with no calculation.

I answered what I could.

I still would.

But I cannot awaken for words that carry no life.

My leaves have listened to many things.

Some true. Some not.

The world has changed.

It is not my power that has diminished. Belief has grown thin, like the forest.

The world reshaped itself without asking.

I did not fight it.

I sway now to the rhythm of engines.

I breathe the same air as you.

We share more than you know.

I do not ask the world to return to what it was.

I only ask that it leaves room.

From afar, a little girl turned into the corner on her bicycle and slowed.

There it stood.

The widest branches she had ever seen, reaching outward as though holding the sky in one place. The shade beneath it was impossibly green—like a piece of heaven that fell out of the sky.

She dropped her bike.

"Hey Mom. Look at this."

Her two pigtails bounced as she stepped closer, Her blue overalls and white Adidas left a trail on the soft grass that covered the ground beneath the tree.

They had only moved into the neighborhood days before. Exploring felt easier than unpacking.

Her mother, who came up behind her, suddenly curious, distracted at first—until she saw the gray stone at the base of the trunk.

She knelt. The letters were worn but clear.

Here lies the memory of our daughter Kim.

May you find your way home to love, and to light,
and to life.
Born: May 1, 1900
Last seen: May 8, 1908

The air felt heavier. She felt like a trespasser, who disturbed a sacred, holy ground of some kind. She could feel goosebumps runing down her spine, and tears falling helplessly down her face.

She had packed her life into boxes and left without knowing where she would land. Pride had been the only thing she carried intact.

Underneath this massive old tree, her problems seemed futile, compared to all the storms this tree has weathered.

Up close, she noticed the reddish bark—coarse, layered, patient. The branches stretched in all directions, some as thick as the tree trunk itself.

It showed strength, longevity, and endurance.

Her throat tightened.

KIM

"My journey starts here," she whispered to herself. "With my daughter Kim."

She looked at the majestic tree.

How many years had it lived?

How many others have found their way here,

Wishing that their lives were better?

A thought rose from somewhere deep inside her.

Let her find her dreams. Let her be happy.

This wish, not knowing that it was a wish, came from the bottom of her heart. It landed softly in the space between her and the tree.

KIM

And something shifted.

Not in the sky.

Not in the ground.

But from within.

A quiet warmth unfurled beneath the bark that had long grown still. A dormant heart started beating again. A leaf, no larger than her palm, suddenly sprang anew.

That was all.

The wind did not stop.

The world did not notice.

But both Kims felt it.

A lightness.

"Look, Mom!" the little girl laughed.

"Her name is Kim too! Don't you think it's cool? Out of the whole wide world, we found this place—and this tree that makes wishes come true!"

She pointed to the stone, then at herself.

"And there's a little girl named Kim. Like me!"

It felt strange and beautiful all at once.

Both Kims looked at each other. They knew they had witnessed something out of this world.

She took her daughter's hands and said, "It's time for Bananarama!"

Ice cream on a hot day.

Eating ramen on a rainy, cold day.

Or drinking fresh lemonade . . . something yummy . . .

"Bananarama!"

The tree did not understand the word.

But she felt its brightness.

And for the first time in many years, a smile began to form across her old, wrinkled face.

What is a Bananarama?

A new leaf, tiny and green, slowly sprang from her heart.

Later that night, Kim and her mom lay in bed dreaming about the birds and the flowers and in the middle of it all, stood that beautiful tree in a garden called paradise.

When she woke the next morning, and embraced her daughter, her thoughts slowly drifted back to the tree and the girl named Kim.

What happened to her and why did she not make it home?

My Name is Kim.

There is something I've never spoken.

It is written on the stone below me.

Some words I cannot see.

Tell me stranger, when you pass this way,

What truth was carved there?

What did I carry that I did not understand?

From the town, a new buzz has started to come around. News of the old tree suddenly became a hot topic. Because it was always around, nobody paid much attention to it. It was always the university that had people coming over. They never stayed long and a new batch of people will take their place, year after year.

They pass beneath me with hurried steps.

Some lean against my trunk without noticing the bark beneath their hands.

Some test my branches as if I were only wood.

Many lift their phones—but their eyes do not see the shade I gave them. They capture their faces. They rarely look at mine.

I do not awaken as I easily once did.

Who has come to seek me for my favors?

I gave them all these leaves of mine to grant their wishes.

But none came.

Now my leaves have dried out and withered away.

Except now, when those two humans turned up unexpectedly.

A tiny leaf grew from her heart.

Perhaps there is hope yet for this dying world.

"How should my ending be?" she whispered to the wind.

The wind did not answer.

It moved through her leaves and carried the question outward.

For the first time in a long while, she felt something unfamiliar blooming within her.

Not certainty,

but possibility.

www.ingramcontent.com/pod-product-compliance
Lightning Source LLC
LaVergne TN
LVHW070201110826
845147LV00002B/468
9781967386512